Spending Time With My Grandparents
Authors: Chantal Magracia & Sarah Ouldzini
AF268874
Spending Time With My Grandparents 1

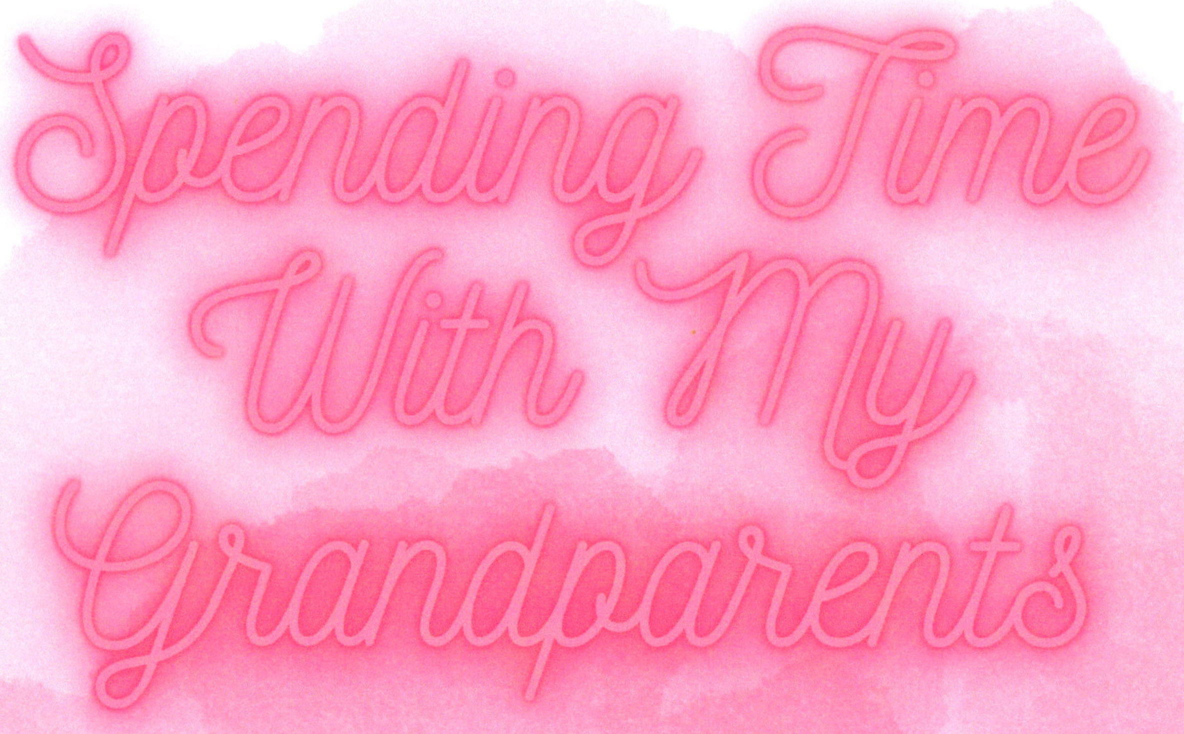

Authors:
Chantal V. Magracia - Ouldzini
Sarah Ouldzini

First published in Canada in 2022
by Chantal Magracia of PhilMorCan Press.
Copyright © 2022 Chantal Magracia
ISBN: 978-1-7772044-3-3

This book is a gift for:

____

This book is a gift from:

____

This way to the garden →

Hi friends!

My name is Arabella and I'd love to share with you how I spend time with my grandparents!

I love biking to my grandparents' house to visit my Lolo and Lola whenever I can. They are two of my most favorite people in the whole world. I love spending time with them so I always make time for them.

"Lolo" means "Grandpa" AND "Lola" means "Grandma".

My Lolo is the best gardener I know! He's the King of the Garden! He takes really good care of his plants and flowers. He spends so much time on them. Lolo knows how much I love sunflowers! Every year, I help him plant so many of them.

Hi Lolo! How can I help you today?
I brought you some goodies from Mom's garden!

Hello Arabella! I'm so happy you came by today! Thanks to you and your mom!
Of course! You're more than welcome to come and help me plant these seeds anytime!

My Lolo is a retired carpenter and he can build anything and everything from scratch! This year, he built a sunflower swing just for me! It's so beautiful and I love it so much. "Salamat po, Lolo!"

"Salamat po, Lolo," means "Thank you, Grandpa!"

Today, I can show you how to build a swing and make sunflower oil for your Lola's cooking!
Yay! I'm so excited, Lolo! I can't wait to help you and learn from you!
Spending Time With My Grandparents 10

Sometimes, my Lolo even delivers some freshly picked sunflowers right to our doorstep because he knows that sunflowers can brighten up anyone's day!

Arabella, are you ready to work hard today, my apo?
Always po, Lolo! I'm ready whenever you are! My basket's ready too!
"Apo" means "grandchild".
"po" is said to show respect to the elderly.

The Next Day

At my Lolo and Lola's house, my Lolo and Lola greeted me with tight hugs and showered me with kisses!

I hope you're ready to work hard today, my apo! We'll be baking a lot all day and I'm excited to teach you my recipes!
"Apo" means "grandchild".
Spending Time With My Grandparents 14

"po" is said to show respect to the elderly.

On the weekends, my Lola greets us with the scent of delicious, freshly baked pastries. I always compliment her efforts, "Ang sarap naman po, Lola. Salamat po, Lola!"

"Ang sarap naman po, Lola," means "This tastes delicious, Grandma."
"Salamat po, Lola," means "Thank you, Grandma!"

My Lola can make anything and everything from scratch! She's the Queen of the Kitchen and she's truly the best pâtissière and chocolatier I know!

Today, we made chocolate
strawberry cake together,
"Salamat po, Lola!"
"Salamat po, Lola," means "Thank you, Grandma!"

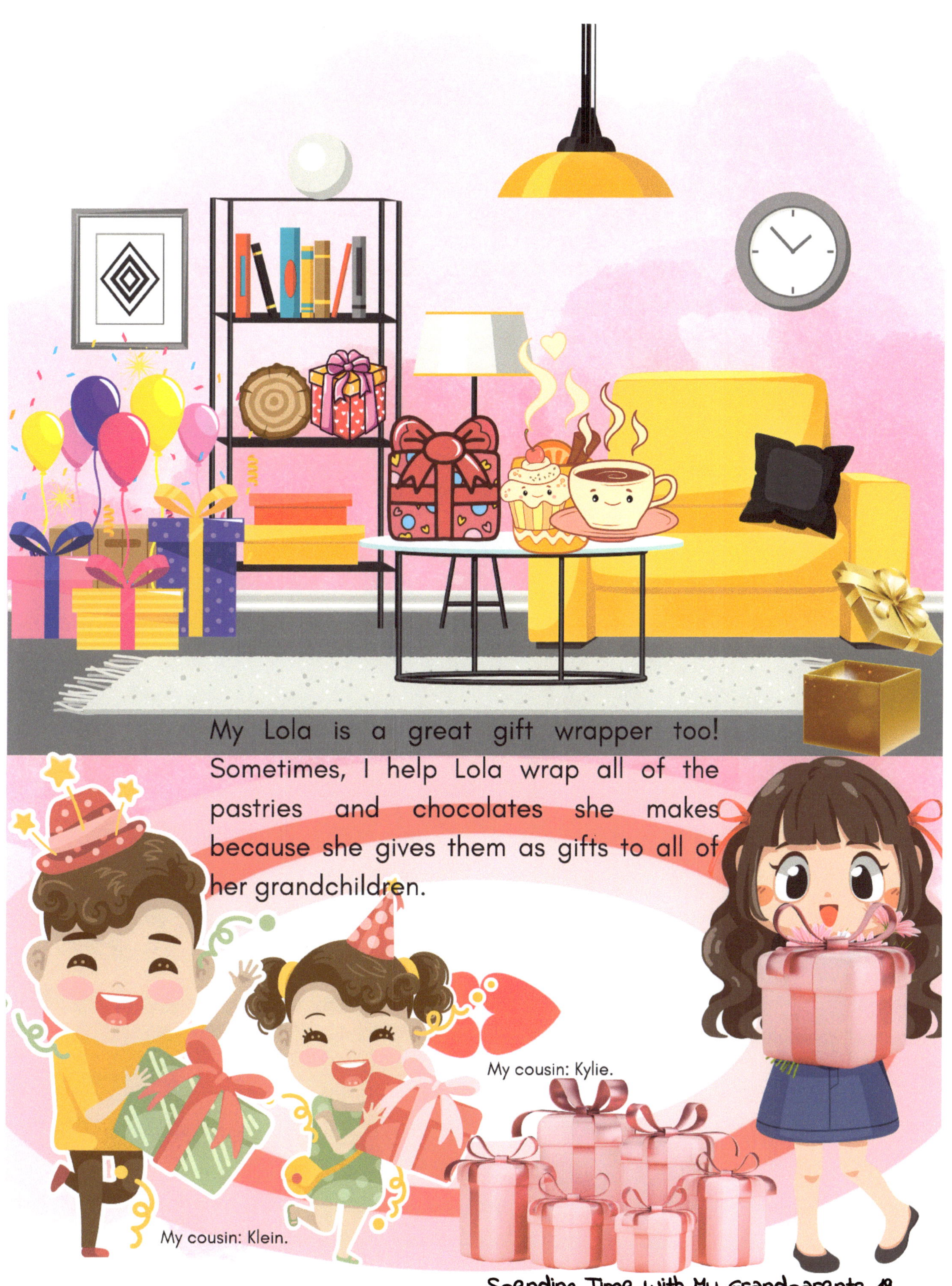

My Lola is a great gift wrapper too! Sometimes, I help Lola wrap all of the pastries and chocolates she makes because she gives them as gifts to all of her grandchildren.

My cousin: Kylie.

My cousin: Klein.

I love reading so much - all thanks to my Lolo and Lola! Both of them love to read stories to me, at least 20 minutes a day. At the end of each story, they always ask me who, what, when, where, why, which, and how questions. I fell in love with reading, so I borrow a lot of books from the library!

Spending Time With My Grandparents 21

"Apo" means "grandchild".
"Of course, apo. I would love to read to you, Arabella. Today, I have an hour to read with you! Let's go read together!"

After a hard day's work, we usually play a game of checkers or chess to relax.

Thanks to my Lolo and Lola, I've become really good at checkers.

I'm still learning how to play chess though.

We enjoy this game before we go to sleep.

I think that my Love Language is both "Quality Time" and "Acts of Service".

Because I feel loved the most when my grandparents spend quality time with me.

I also feel loved the most when my grandparents go out of their way for me - they always go above and beyond!

That's also how I show them that I love them and care for them is when I spend time with them and when I make time to help them out whenever I can!

"po" is said to show respect to the elderly.

Spending Time with My Grandparents 24

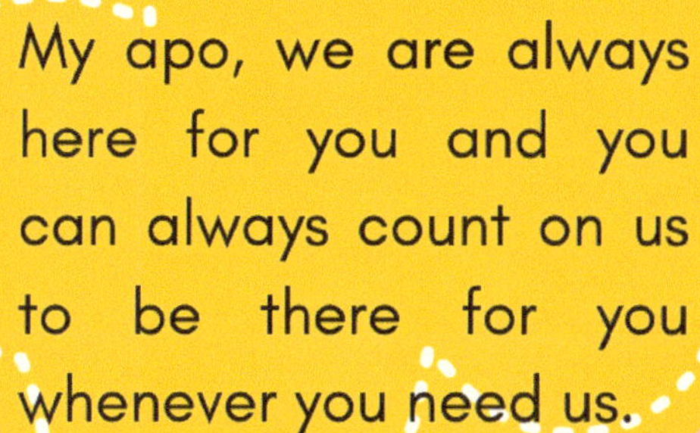

My apo, we are always here for you and you can always count on us to be there for you whenever you need us.
Oh my beloved Arabella, you are our most precious grandchild and we would always make time for you. I love you unconditionally with all my heart and soul!

To Our Dearly Beloved Apo,

We love you with the kind of love
that you can trust.
We love you with the kind of love
that you can depend on.
We love you with the kind of love
that will protect you.
We love you with the kind of love
that will never betray you.

We're extremely lucky and blessed
to have you in our lives and us in yours.
We're extremely grateful
to you and for you.
Always.

"Apo" means "grandchild".

I love spending so much time with my grandparents because I always learn so many new things from them!

How about you? What are some of the things you like to do with your grandparents?

Spending Time with My Grandparents 26

Spending Time With My Grandparents

Hello friends,

Here are some things that I like to do when I spend time with my grandparents. How about you? What are some of the things you like to do with your grandparents? How do you make your grandparents feel appreciated, cared for, and loved? How do you show them that you are grateful for them and grateful to them? I always do the best that I can to make my grandparents feel all of that and more! I love them to the moon and infinity!

Love Always,
Arabella

Chantal Magracia is a Filipino-Canadian author, educator, entrepreneur, and philanthropist, who graduated with a Bachelor of Education degree from the University of Alberta. She is currently pursuing higher education from the University of British Columbia.

She is an experienced teacher who has taught K-12 students, including adult learners since 2011 in Alberta, Canada. She is a permanently licensed educator both in Alberta, Canada and British Columbia, Canada.

She has always been extremely passionate about Character Education which encompasses values, principles, ethics, morals, virtues, good manners, right conduct, and proper etiquette. In her work, she is highly driven to model what empathy, compassion, kindness, acceptance, consideration, thoughtfulness, and understanding looks like in our daily lives. She's a dedicated and devoted life-long learner with great work ethics, who prefers to write children's books as her medium of choice, to share her learnings, reflections, epiphanies, wisdom, and growth regarding her constant pursuit of becoming the best version of herself simply by helping and uplifting others.